The Little Shepherd

Introduction

This beautiful story first came into my life as a little Christmas gift from a special friend. For many years at that sacred time of commemoration of the birth of Jesus, I have read its inspiring lines to family, friends, and hundreds of students. All have enjoyed and cherished its special message. Now I take distinct pleasure in sharing it once again with the world.

Margaret E. Sangster wrote it under the original title, *Anniversary*. May God bless her for sharing her talent and good spirit through this heart touching, inspired writing.

It was first published in December, 1936, *Good Housekeeping Magazine*.

The Little Shepherd

The little boy sat quite alone on the hilltop, his shepherd's crook across his knees, his small square lunch basket beside him. He made an odd distorted shadow in the white light of the moon, for even the shawl that his mother had woven of lamb's wool could not hide the ugly hump that lay between his shoulders.

Far below him, dotting the hillside with irregular shadows, were the sheep. The majority of them slept, but a few wandered aimlessly up and down the slope. The little boy, however, was not watching the flock. His head was thrown back, and his wide eyes were fixed on the sky. There was an intensity in his gaze and a strange wistful smile on his lips.

The boy was thinking, "Perhaps it will happen again. Perhaps, though a third of a century has gone by, I shall be privileged to see the great star and hear the angel voices as my father did."

The moon, riding high in the heavens, went under a black cloud. For a moment the world was dark. The little boy sighed and lowered his eyes. "Though it is the time of anniversary," he breathed, "there will be no star this night. Neither will the angels sing..."

The time of anniversary. How often he had listened to the story of the miracle that had taken place so long ago! The little boy's father had been a little boy then—he had been the youngest of the shepherds on that glorious occasion when an angel anthem sounded across the world and a star shone over the tranquil town of Bethlehem. His father had followed that star; with other shepherds he had come to the stable of the inn. Crowding through the narrow doorway he had seen a woman with a baby in her arms.

"But," his father would say, "she was no ordinary woman! There was something in her face that made one think of a...lighted candle. And there was a tenderness in her smile that the very cattle felt, for they drew near to her, and seemed to even kneel. It was not completely her beauty—although beauty she did possess! It was a shine from within."

"And the baby... what of the baby?" the little boy would ask.

The father's hand habitually touched his small son's shoulder at this point— touched it and drew away as if the brief contact cause him anguish; the hump,

4

high and distorted, was so obvious.

"The baby," he said, and his voice grew hushed, "was as unlike other infants as his mother was different from other women. Scarce an hour old when first I glimpsed him, yet there was a sense of wisdom on his brow, and his tiny, up-curled hands seemed so tender, yet even then to hold power. I found myself kneeling as the cattle knelt, and there was moisture upon my face; and though I was a lad tall for my age—I was not ashamed."

Alone on the hillside, the little boy could almost hear the sound of his father's voice in the stillness; his father's voice telling the story of the marvelous infant and of the Wise Men who had come to visit, following the path of the star. They had come bearing gifts, the fame of which traveled through all the land. Often he had heard of the gold and frankincense and myrrh and he had shivered at the tale of the great, but cruel, king who had ordered death to all the infants. Often he had thrilled to the danger and excitement of a worried young mother and her sober husband who had stolen away into the land of Egypt with their child.

"Many of us thought that the child had been captured and slain by Herod," the little boy's father invariably finished, "until a decade passed and we heard rumors of a youth who bore his name, who lectured in a temple at Jerusalem to a group of learned doctors. A few years ago we heard that this same youth, now grown older, had organized a group of men; that with them he was journeying from place to place preaching, teaching, and aiding the needy. "And," (here the little boy's father had a habit of lowering his voice and glancing seriously around the room), "there are some who say he has become a Messiah, and that he does more than just help the cause of the common people. There are some who say that he performs wonderful deeds—healing the sick, and the blind, and the lepers—even raising the dead."

Once at this point the little boy interrupted, "Oh, I would that I might meet him. I would that he might take the hump from my back and make me strong and straight like other children."

With a loving finger laid against her son's lips, the little boy's mother warned silence. "What must be must be," she told him. "You were born that way, my son. It is better," looking at her husband, "that we change the subject! There might be listening ears."

It was growing cold on the hillside. The child drew the shawl closer about his tired body and wished that he were not a shepherd. Shepherds led a lonely life—they did not fit into the bright places of the world. Rooms that were gaily lighted at eventide were for men and boys who worked hard by day and earned their moments of ease; they were not for shepherds. But what else could a crippled boy do besides tend sheep?

Yawning wearily, the little boy looked up at the sky. From the position of the moon he judged it to be about middle night. It was still a long while before sunrise; still hours before someone would come to take his place and he could limp home. Yet middle night had its good too! For at that time he could break his fast and partake of the lunch his mother had packed so neatly into a basket.

As he reached for the basket, and opened it slowly, the little boy was wondering what had been prepared for him tonight by his mother. He found a flask of goat's milk, and nearly a loaf of crusty, dark bread, and some yellow cheese. He also found dried figs, sugary with their own sweetness. Wrapped separately, he came upon a real treat—a cake made of eggs and sifted flour with lemon in it—and raisins!

He had expected the bread, and the cheese, and the milk. Even the figs he had expected. But the cake was a surprise—the sort of surprise that happened seldom to break the monotony of watching his father's sheep. His eyes gleamed as he surveyed it and some of the sadness went out of him. Carefully he set the basket down and spread on the ground beside him the square of linen in which his mother had folded the lunch. Carefully he laid out the flask of milk, the bread, the cheese, but not the cake, which he left tucked away in the depths of the basket. He left it there so he might not be tempted to eat it first!

"It is so good to be hungry," he said aloud. "Yes, and to have food."

Suddenly, from somewhere just behind him, a voice spoke. It was not a loud voice and yet it seemed to carry beyond the hillside.

"Indeed, yes," said the voice. "It is good to be hungry and to have food and to. . ."

Startled, for he thought he was quite alone with his thoughts and the drowsing sheep, the little boy glanced back across his crooked shoulder. He saw a man standing upon the brow of the hill, silhouetted against the moonlit sky. Ordinarily he would have been afraid, for there were sometimes cruel robbers in the middle of the night. But somehow the sight of this man, who was tall and muscular, failed to frighten him. He did not know why he instinctively completed the man's unfinished sentence.

"And to share it," he murmured. "You are a stranger, sir?"

The man came closer to the child and stood looking down on him. "No, not a stranger," he said slowly, "never a stranger. As it happens, my journey started not far from this very place, started years before you saw the light, my lad. I am on my way to complete the circle."

Although he couldn't imagine what the man meant, the boy made swift response.

"I was about to eat my lunch," he said, pointing at the square of linen on which he had arranged the food from his basket. "One grows hungry on the hillside. I am a shepherd, sir. I tend my father's flock, and each night my mother packs for me a simple meal. Will you be seated—and break bread with me?"

The boy hesitated shyly, "Perhaps you will talk with me as we eat? It grows lonely on the dark hillside. I long at times for companionship."

The man continued to peer down from his impressive height. His eyes held a warm glow. It was as if a candle burned somewhere behind them, the little boy thought. He recalled words that his father had spoken when he described a woman in a stable. He felt so comforted by the man's glance that he smiled up into the kindly face, and the man spoke again.

"It is a strange coincidence," he said, "the fact that you are a shepherd, for I also tend my father's flock! And I also. . ." his face shown with a luminous smile, "have often grown lonely waiting for the gates of dawn to open. Are you sure," the man began to gracefully seat himself upon the ground, "that you have sufficient nourishment for two? I should not like to deprive you of anything."

Gazing, fascinated, into the man's face, the little boy replied, "But yes! I have

a large flask of goat's milk, and some
yellow cheese, nearly a loaf of bread and
ten figs. And, "—for a second he
hesitated—"that's a great plenty," he
finished. He did not mention the cake,
still wrapped in the basket. For a cake—a
cake made of sifted flour, and eggs, and
lemon and raisins—was indeed a rare
delicacy. And it was not a very big cake.

The man bent forward to re-tie the
thong of his sandal. The little boy saw
that the sandal was covered with dust.
He tried to keep his eyes from glancing
toward his lunch basket as he tore the
crusty brown bread into fragments.

"Perhaps your feet are aching," he said
as he placed the fragments in the center
of the linen cloth. "This hill is hard to
climb. I am close to being spent when
I reach the summit of it, but I must
needs sit high so I can watch all the
sheep."

The man said slowly, "I have climbed
steeper hills than this, my lad, and know
there are steeper hills to come. My feet
do not ache. How long,"—abruptly

changing the subject—"have you been crippled?"

The little boy would have resented such a display of curiosity if the inquiry had come from an ordinary person. But for this man the question seemed a natural one, to be answered naturally.

"Why," he said, "I have never been without a hump between my shoulders. I hate it, but. . ."—and he began to quote his mother—"what must be, must be!" Then his childish face became a trifle unchildish. "Still, it is hard to go through life looking like one of the camels that the wise men rode when they came from the East with their caravans—"

The man interrupted, "What, lad? You know of the wise men from the East? How does it happen that you should mention them to me on this night? It is very curious!" The man began to partake of a piece of the crusty dark bread.

Laughing softly, the little boy answered, "I suppose the wise men are in my mind because this is the time of anniversary, and I have been thinking of the baby that was born in a stable. I was hoping—before you arrived—that once again the great star might shine and the angels might sing. I have, in fact, been watching the sky rather than the sheep."

The man asked another swift question. "What do you know about these holy things—about the star and the song? You are so very young!"

The little boy exclaimed, "All Bethlehem heard about the star, and the infant who lay in the manger because there was no room at the inn... I know, perhaps more than the others, for my father, a child then, was one of the shepherds who saw the light from the heavens and heard the angel music. Will you..." the little boy had taken the flask of goat's milk in his hands, "will you share with me this cup, sir? For, perhaps you thirst."

The man took the flask from the lad's small hands. His fingers were powerful, and yet as gentle as a woman's. He said,

"I will share this cup with you lad, for I *do* thirst."

Then he watched the man drink deeply. The little boy thought it must be tiring to tramp from place to place.

He said, on impulse, as the stranger set down the flask, "Will you tell me, sir, of some of the towns in which you have stayed?"

The man answered, "Ah yes, my lad, I have seen many towns—Capernaum, Nazareth, Jerusalem, and many many others. Each has some good and some bad. Each has some poverty and pain rubbing shoulders with wealth and ease. In every city I have found health on one hand and illness on the other—and in each city more deeds to be done than one short lifetime can accommodate."

"Why sir, you are still young and strong. You have many years left. How old are you sir? I turned ten in the spring," the boy added.

The man's voice was muted as he replied, "I am more than three times your age lad."

"When is your time of birth, sir?" the boy asked suddenly.

The man smiled his beautiful, luminous smile. "It's odd that you should ask, dear lad, for this is my day of birth. You, quite unknowingly, are giving me an anniversary feast—and never has a feast been more welcomed. I was weary and forlorn when I came upon you."

"Weary and forlorn!" the little boy queried. "Haven't you any people of your own? People with whom you can be happy on the day of your birth? When my birthday arrives, mother prepares a real feast for me and gives me gifts. This shawl I wear, have you noted it? She wove it for my last birthday."

The man reached over and rested his hand on the little boy's knee. "I fear," he said, "my loved ones are not near enough just now to celebrate with me. But maybe there will be a gift for me at my journey's end."

The little boy's knee felt a tingle under the pressure of the friendly hand. He asked, "When, sir, shall you come to your journey's end?"

The man did not meet the child's gaze, but solemnly replied, "Perhaps very soon!"

The little boy looked worried. He said, "You don't look happy about it. Don't you want to come to the end of your travels? Don't you want to reach home and see what gift they have for you?"

The man hesitated ever so slightly. "Yes," he said at last, "I want to reach home. But the gift, it may be too beautiful to bear; or too heavy for me to carry. I suppose," his face looked pensive in the white moonlight, "I should be getting on, but you have made this birthday very wonderful, my lad."

Peeping down at the white cloth with its remnants of bread and cheese, the little boy thought, "There seems to be as much as ever. He couldn't have liked it." Slantwise he contemplated the man's face, and suddenly he was swept with a burning sense of shame. The boy cried out, one word tumbling over the other,

"You did not enjoy your food, sir! You have not had a true birthday feast. That is because I have been selfish and mean!" In a confessing tone, the boy continued, "I have a cake in my basket; a cake I was saving to eat alone, after you left. It is a cake of sifted flour and eggs and lemon and raisins, and I love cake! But now," the little boy's voice quivered, "I would not enjoy it if I ate it all alone, sir. I have desire to give the cake to you—as my birthday gift to you. Perhaps you will eat it later, when the chill of early morning has set in, and you are on the road."

The man did not speak. His eyes were like stars now, instead of candles, as he watched his small host lift the cake from the basket and display its rich goodness. It was only when the lad extended it toward him that he broke into speech.

"Ah, my lad," he said, "you have sustained me with your bread, and we have drunk deep of the same cup. And now, we will share this cake, which shall be, through your bounty, my birthday cake. We will apportion it equally, and we will eat of it together, you and I. And, as I walk alone along the road, I shall remember a little lad's generosity."

Gravely, as if he were handling something infinitely precious, the man took the rich cake into his fingers. Carefully he divided it so the two sections were equal, and said, "Bless unto us this food, my Father." The little boy was startled, for there was no one else upon the hillside. Then the man continued, "This is the cake of life, lad. Enjoy it to the last crumb." So he and the little boy ate the cake together, and the little boy thought he had never tasted such good food. It was as if the cake's richness were, verily, the richness of life! As he licked the last crumbs from his fingers, he felt as if he were gathering force and vigor and purpose. In his mind, for no reason at all, he saw a picture of himself, big and handsome and brave, striding down the road with his weakness, the ugly hump, cast from him.

"It's like a vision," he said aloud. But when the man asked, "What do you mean, lad?" the boy hung his head and was unable to answer.

Indeed, he was silent so long that the man's hand came to rest lightly upon his shoulder—lightly, but oh so firmly! There was something in the touch that made tears hang on the little boy's eyelashes.

"Oh," he cried, "do not leave me, sir! We could be such friends, you and me. Come with me to my home and dwell with my family. My mother will bake many cakes for you, and my father will share with you of his plenty. And I, you can have my bed, and even this fringed shawl that I wear. Oh, do not journey on, sir! Stay with me, here in... Bethlehem."

The man spoke, his voice like a great bell tolling over hill and valley. "I must go on. I must be about my Father's business. But I shall never leave you, my lad. Lo, I am with you always, even unto the end of the world!"

Bowing his head in his hands, covering his misted eyes, the little boy was

aware of the man's firm fingers travel-
ing up from his shoulder until they
touched his hair. But now he couldn't
speak, for a pulse drummed in his
throat. When he raise his head, the man
was gone, and the hillside empty, save
for the shadows of the sheep, which
were asleep.

The little boy sobbed once, sharply,
with a sense of loss and then struggled
to his feet. Only, he didn't have to strug-
gle really, for there was a curious
lightness about his body, and a feeling
of freshness and peace—a peace that
transcended the pain of parting. But it
was not until he pulled his fringed
lamb's wool shawl tighter across his
back, that he realized how straight he
was standing, and how straight he would
now always stand.

The Beginning.